My Princess Collection

Mulan

The Highest Honor

Book Three

Written by M. L. Dunham

For information address Disney Press, 114 Fifth Avenue,
New York, New York 10011-5690.
First Edition
Printed in China
5 7 9 10 8 6
ISBN 0-7868-4596-1

For more Disney Press fun,
visit www.disneybooks.com

Chapter One

My name is Fa Mulan. I am here to tell you my story. It is a story about family, my family, the Fa family. It is the story of my love for my father.

It all began when the Huns attacked our country, China. In times of war, men are called to fight for our country. Sometimes, if a father is called but is too weak to fight, his son may volunteer to take his place. In my family, I am an only child, and I am female. When my father was called off to war, my heart was broken. He had fought bravely in a previous war, and he had been injured. He would not survive another battle. I did not know what to do.

So, I decided I would pretend to be his son and take his place. One night, as a storm raged outside, I cut off my hair and put on my father's armor.

I took my father's conscription notice from my parents' bedside, and in its place I left my comb, so they would know where I had gone. I did not want to tell them my plan ahead of time because I knew they would try to stop me.

Then I saddled my horse, Khan, and rode off to meet the army.

Chapter Two

My ancestors sent a little dragon named Mushu to watch over me. He, Khan, and a lucky cricket named Cri-Kee accompanied me. When we reached the army camp, I encountered many troubles.

The men thought I was one of them. They wanted to fight with me and treat me like a man. I did everything I could to avoid it— but sometimes I ended up getting everyone, including myself, into trouble.

I was weaker than the others, but I tried
very hard during our training. Still, I seemed
to fail miserably at almost everything I
attempted. It wasn't easy being a soldier.

One day, we were running through the mountains with weights across our shoulders. Our captain, Shang, wanted us to be strong so we would be prepared for battle. But the weights were heavy, and I could barely keep up with the others. At last, I tripped, falling to the ground. Captain Shang saw me. He picked up my weights, carrying double the load of anyone else. I was humiliated as I pulled myself to my feet. I was failing as a soldier, and I knew it.

Then one day, Captain Shang shot an arrow into the top of a tall pole. He asked us to climb the pole, carrying two heavy weights.

"This," he said, pointing to one of the weights, "represents discipline." Then he pointed to the other weight. "And this represents strength. You need both to reach the arrow."

No one could do it. But I was determined, and I thought long and hard about the task. At last, I figured out a way to loop the weights together to climb the pole. When I reached the top, everyone cheered. Even Shang looked pleased.

Chapter Three

One day, we were called to help our fellow countrymen fight in battle. As we crossed a snow-covered mountain range to join them, we were attacked by the Huns.

I managed to help our troops defeat the
Huns by causing an avalanche. And I also
saved Captain Shang's life.

Unfortunately, I was injured while saving him. When I was unconscious, the army doctor who examined me discovered my secret.

"I did it for my father," I tried to explain. But Shang felt betrayed.

"A life for a life," he finally said, throwing down his sword. "My debt is repaid." He was sparing my life because I had saved his. But I was no longer welcome as a soldier in his army. They left me shivering and alone in the snow-covered mountains.

Chapter Four

After the others had left, I saw some Huns emerge from the snow where they had been buried by the avalanche. Among them was Shan-Yu, their horrible and vicious leader. I knew I had to warn Shang and the others, so I raced to the city where they were meeting with the Emperor. They did not realize Shan-Yu was hiding, ready to attack!

When I found Shang and the others, no one would believe my story. Soon, the worst happened: Shan-Yu captured the Emperor and held him captive in the palace. Shan-Yu and his men locked all the entrances. No one could get inside to help the Emperor.

Finally, I managed to convince some of my army friends to help. Even Shang eventually joined me. I formulated a plan, to disguise the men as women. The Huns would never expect women to attack them. Soon we managed to defeat Shan-Yu and save the Emperor—using cleverness, not strength.

Chapter Five

The Emperor was grateful, but I figured he would be angry with me for pretending I was a man in order to save my father. Instead, he thanked me. And he honored my family.

"Take this," he said, handing me his
pendant, "so your family will know what you
have done for me." Then he handed me
Shan-Yu's sword. "And take this so the world
will know what you have done for China."

Then I rode off, back to my family.

When I returned home, my family was so happy to see me safe and sound. They were deeply honored by the Emperor's gifts.

And as for Shang, he found out where I lived, and he came to see me. I liked that part. In fact, I asked him, "Would you like to stay for dinner?"

And I felt very much in agreement with Grandmother Fa when she added, "Would you like to stay forever?"